LITTLE LUIS AND THE BAD BANDIT

"A fast-forward adventure of goodies versus baddies and love conquering all." *The Independent on Sunday*

It's brain versus brawn when Little Luis takes on Mexican Pete! This funny and highly entertaining story is perfect for young readers.

Ann Jungman trained as a lawyer, then taught in primary schools for ten years, before becoming a full-time writer of children's books. She has now written over seventy titles, including the popular Vlad the Drac stories, which have been broadcast on BBC Radio 5.

Russell Ayto was shortlisted for the Smarties Book Prize and the Mother Goose Award for his first picture book, *Quacky Quack-quack!* He has also illustrated the Walker picture books *Lazy Jack* and *Mrs Potter's Pig* and the fiction title *Broops! Down the Chimney*.

Some other titles

Art, You're Magic!
by Sam McBratney

Beware Olga!
by Gillian Cross

Holly and the Skyboard
by Ian Whybrow

Jolly Roger
by Colin McNaughton

Millie Morgan, Pirate
by Margaret Ryan

Pappy Mashy
by Kathy Henderson

The Snow Maze
by Jan Mark

Tillie McGillie's Fantastical Chair
by Vivian French

The Unknown Planet
by Jean Ure

ANN JUNGMAN

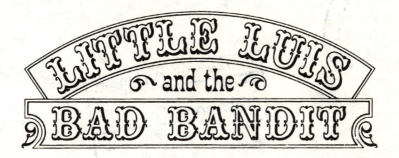

LITTLE LUIS and the BAD BANDIT

Illustrations by Russell Ayto

WALKER BOOKS
AND SUBSIDIARIES
LONDON · BOSTON · SYDNEY

For Freddie
A.J.

First published 1993 by Walker Books Ltd
87 Vauxhall Walk, London SE11 5HJ

This edition published 1994

4 6 8 10 9 7 5 3

Text © 1993 Ann Jungman
Illustrations © 1993 Russell Ayto

Printed in England

British Library Cataloguing in Publication Data
A catalogue record for this book is
available from the British Library.

ISBN 0-7445-3189-6

Contents

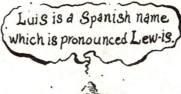

Luis is a Spanish name which is pronounced Lew-is.

Mexican Pete

Long ago in Mexico there lived
a wicked bandit called Mexican
Pete. Mexican Pete had the longest
mustachios and the biggest sombrero
in all of Mexico and everyone was
afraid of him.

Everywhere there were posters
offering a big reward to the person
who captured Mexican Pete.

When the bandit saw the posters,
he just laughed and took out two of
his many guns and fired into the air.

People saw the grim pictures of
Mexican Pete looking down on
them from the walls,
and shook with
fear. Only one
person was not
afraid of Mexican
Pete – and that
was Little Luis.

Luis was the son of the local landowner, Don Francisco Emilio de Garcia y Lopez. Every day, when Little Luis passed the poster of the bandit on his way to church and again on his way back, he would look at the picture and say:

Oh, this Señor Pete has such sad eyes. He is not a happy man.

His father, Don Francisco, did
not agree.

Little Luis wept into his soup.

"Why are you crying?" demanded
his father. "Is it because I have had
more cows stolen?"

Just then Isabella, Little Luis's sister, swept downstairs. She was so beautiful she was known as the Fair Isabellita.

"It must be that bandit!" yelled her father, slamming his fist on the table. "This will have to stop. I will double the reward. Someone is bound to betray him."

Don Francisco was making so much noise that he didn't hear the sounds of people marching and shouting. Luis and Isabellita did and ran to the window.

"Papa," Little Luis said, "it is the villagers. They are all coming this way and they look very upset."

"It's that bandit, I'll be bound," declared his father. "Let them come in."

Soon the room was full of people all talking at once.

"Quiet," Don Francisco commanded. "One at a time. Now, Maria, what is it?"

"Oh, Don Francisco, all the water melons I collected to sell in the market have been stolen. Oh, how will I feed my eight children?"

"Dry your tears, Maria," said Don Francisco. "Here is money for food."

"Now, Pancho. What has happened to you?"

"Don Francisco, both my goats have been stolen and there is no milk for anyone."

"More work of Mexican Pete, I warrant," said Don Francisco. "Pancho, take one of my goats."

"And old Ramirez, what has this bandit taken of yours?"

"My medals from the war, Don Francisco, the one I fought in with your father. They were my pride and joy."

"Ramirez, don't cry. I will give you the medals that were my father's. Now, everyone listen: I, Don Francisco Emilio de Garcia y Lopez, promise you that soon this Mexican Pete will stop stealing from us."

The people cheered and went home feeling comforted.

Little Luis thought to himself, "This Señor Pete, now he's stealing from the poor people. It will not do! My father can afford to lose some cattle and my sister can live without her jewels, but Maria's children cannot eat if her fruit is stolen."

Little Luis

The next day Little Luis stared at the
poster of Mexican Pete for a bit
longer than usual. All around,
people were talking about the thefts
and shaking their fists at the picture.

No one noticed that under a
nearby tree a stranger lay asleep.
He had a blanket over him and
his sombrero covered his face.

For one moment he raised his hat
and took a peep. It was only for a
second, but when Little Luis saw his
eyes he knew the stranger was
none other than Mexican Pete.

Little Luis turned and said to Old
Ramirez, who was very deaf:

And Little Luis returned home, smiling to himself.

The next day, on his way to church, Little Luis suddenly felt an arm round him and then found himself lifted on to a horse. It was the wicked bandit!

Mexican Pete rode like lightning to his hideout. There he dumped Little Luis on the ground.

"You're nothing but a pipsqueak. All right, pipsqueak, go and collect some wood. We need a fire."

Little Luis put out his hand and
patted the bandit's horse. Suddenly,
without any warning, the horse
reared up and ...

dumped Mexican Pete into the river.

Little Luis helped him out.

"Come on, Señor Pete, take my hand. Now you get those wet clothes off quickly and I will dry them on this rock."

So the bandit took off his soaking clothes and, growling, put on a new set. Then he climbed onto his horse.

Again Little Luis patted the horse and again the horse reared up…

and threw Mexican Pete into a pile of mud.

"Oh, Señor Pete!" cried Little Luis. "You are covered in mud. Take off these clothes and I will wash them in the river."

Little Luis trooped off with the
dirty clothes, but before he went he
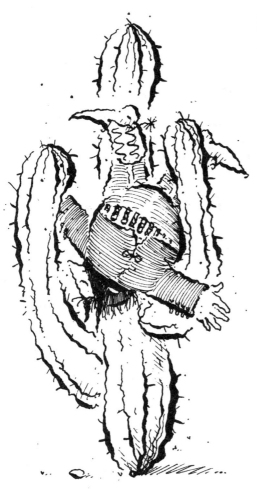
put a thorn
under the
saddle.

Mexican
Pete, dressed
in his last set
of clothes,
mounted his
horse. The
horse trotted a
short distance
and then flung
Mexican Pete
against a very
spiky cactus.

"Oh, poor Señor Pete," cried Little
Luis. "You are having no luck today.
I think maybe you should forget
about stealing our supper. No doubt
there is something in the cave that I
can cook."

"That horse is going crazy," the bandit muttered.

"It looks like it," agreed Little Luis. "What a good thing I am here to help, Señor Pete."

That night Little Luis and the bandit ate a simple meal of tortillas.

Mexican Pete was miserable.
To cheer himself up he picked up
his guitar and sang. Little Luis was
amazed to hear
such a glorious
voice. It set him
thinking: a
voice like this
should not
just be heard
by the cactus
and the birds.
Oh, how the
people in the
village would
love to hear
this singing.

35

"Oh, Señor Pete," said Little Luis, wiping away a tear. "My sister will be so worried about me. Señor Pete, would you deliver a short note to say that I am well?"

"I wouldn't want such a beautiful girl to worry," said the bandit. "But I might get caught."

"Oh, no, Señor Pete! If you shave off your mustachios and don't wear your very big sombrero, no one would recognize you."

"Shave off the best mustachios in Mexico? You must be crazy!"

"But my poor sister, Señor Pete. What of her?"

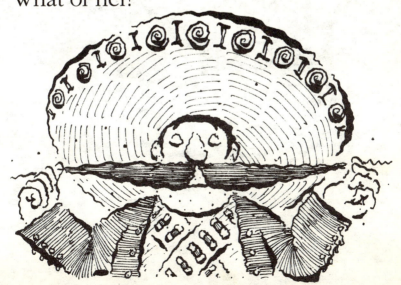

"For the peace of mind of a wonderful girl like that, the sacrifice of my mustachios is a small thing," declared the bandit. "But you must promise not to try to escape."

"Oh, yes! At home I lead a very quiet life. This is exciting. If only I knew that poor Papa and Isabellita were not upset and worried, I would be very happy."

When night fell, the bandit leapt
onto his horse.

Little Luis handed him the note.

"You look very good without the
mustachios, Señor Pete. Now
remember what I told you: if
anyone asks your name, you are
Señor Ernesto Gonzalez."

And so Little Luis waved and
smiled contentedly as the horse
galloped off into the moonlight.

Señor Ernesto

Mexican Pete, in a small sombrero
and without mustachios, rode into
the village. No one recognized him.

Mexican Pete stood under the poster with his picture on it. No one recognized him. Mexican Pete had a drink in the local café. No one recognized him.

All around, people were talking about the kidnapping of Little Luis. Mexican Pete felt bad.

Then Mexican Pete picked up his guitar and went to the house of Don Francisco Emilio de Garcia y Lopez. As he walked through the gardens, he heard the sound of weeping. He looked up and saw the fair Isabellita, in tears. Downstairs, Don Francisco Emilio de Garcia y Lopez sat in despair.

"I make everyone unhappy," said Mexican Pete to himself. "And I am unhappy, too. I must let Isabellita know that her little brother is safe."

Then Mexican Pete began to serenade the fair Isabellita.

In the mountains far away,
A bandit took a boy to stay—
   Olé olé olé olé.

But the boy is well and spry,
He tells his sister
   not to cry—
Olé olé olé olé.

The boy will be home soon,
Well before the next
   full moon—
Olé olé oléeee...
Olé olé oléeeeee!

Isabellita stopped crying and leaned over the balcony.

"Señor, you have seen my brother?"

"Oh, yes, Señorita." Mexican Pete reached up and handed her the note.

"He is the prisoner of the bad bandit. But I, Ernesto Gonzalez, will rescue him."

"Oh, Señor Gonzalez! How happy you have made me!"

Mexican Pete bowed low.

"Señor Gonzalez, when you and Luis come back, will you sing for me again?"

"Señorita, it will be an honour."

Mexican Pete mounted his horse and disappeared into the darkness.

When he got back to camp, Little Luis had steaming coffee all ready. They drank and Mexican Pete said, "I have been a bad man, Little Luis, a very bad man."

Little Luis nodded.

"But the beauty of your sister and the grief of the village people have moved me. Also, I am lonely. I do not like living alone in a cave. My horse keeps going crazy and throwing me into the river and so on."

I will give up being a bandit and become a good man instead.

The next day Señor Ernesto
Gonzalez and Little Luis rode into
the village. When the people saw

Little Luis they cheered. The cheers
brought Isabellita and her father
rushing into the square.

That night there was a great feast, and everyone gathered round while Little Luis told his story.

Mexican Pete tied me up. He was terrible.

Then along came Señor Ernesto Gonzalez and fought Mexican Pete.

Señor Ernesto sang for the crowd.
Everyone loved it, but no one more
than the fair Isabellita.

Señor Ernesto turned out to be a very good man.

On Sundays he sang in the choir,

and in the week he captured wild horses and sold them at a fair price.

He taught the children how to ride and how to sing.

After work he helped people in the fields and in their houses.

Sometimes he even did the washing-up.

"How can we persuade this Señor Ernesto Gonzalez to stay in our village?" the people asked.

Isabellita knew.

The next time Señor Ernesto Gonzalez sang under Isabellita's window, she threw him a flower – which told Señor Ernesto that he could ask for her hand in marriage. Don Francisco was very happy with the idea and later that summer Señor Ernesto Gonzalez and the fair Isabellita were married.

As the couple knelt before the priest, Little Luis gave a sigh. "Oh, I like this Señor Ernesto, who is to be my brother-in-law," he said. "He is a good man!"

MORE WALKER SPRINTERS
For You to Enjoy